GW01033854

BEST FRIENDS

Stories and Poems

Chosen by
June Crebbin

Illustrated by Julie Park

Dent Children's Books
London

For Evelyn

First published in 1990
This selection copyright © June Crebbin, 1990
Illustrations copyright © Julie Park, 1990
All rights reserved

Printed in Great Britain
for J. M. Dent & Sons Ltd
91 Clapham High Street
London SW4 7TA

British Library Cataloguing in Publication Data
Best friends.
   1. Children's short stories in English, 1945–. Anthologies
   I. Crebbin, June II. Park, Julie
823'.01'089282 [J]
ISBN 0–460–88003–9

Contents

Finding a Friend

June Crebbin

'Will you be my friend?'
said the rubbish to the river.
  'No, never.'

'Will you be my friend?'
said the spider to the fly.
  'Not I.'

'Will you be my friend?'
said the lion to the deer.
  'No fear.'

'Will you be my friend?'
said the boat to the sea.
  'Maybe.'

'Will you be my friend?'
said the child to the summer days.
  'Always.'

The Tooth-Ball

Philippa Pearce

Once upon a time there was a boy called Timmy who was sad because he was too shy to make friends.

His grandmother knew this; and she invited him to visit her on her birthday. She wrote to him: 'We'll make a birthday cake. You can blow out the candles and cut the first slice of cake and have my birthday wish for yourself.'

'There!' said Timmy's mother. 'And you can go to Granny's by yourself, on the bus. You're old enough.'

And his father said: 'Don't forget to take your Granny a birthday present.'

So Timmy bought her a box of her favourite chocolates, each chocolate wrapped separately in gold foil.

At his grandmother's, they made the cake and iced it and stuck candles on top and lit them.

Timmy sang, 'Happy birthday to you!' and then blew the candles out.

He began to cut the first slice of cake.

'Don't forget to wish,' said his grandmother.

'I don't believe in wishes,' Timmy said sadly.

'Then I'll wish something for you.'

'What?'

'That's secret. But something special.'

So she wished, as Timmy cut the cake; and they began eating.

Presently Timmy said: 'Here's half an almond.'

'We didn't put any almonds into the cake,' said his grandmother.

'It's not an almond,' said Timmy, examining it. 'It's a tooth. My tooth, that's been wobbling and wobbling. It's come out at last. Was that your special wish, Granny?'

But his grandmother wouldn't say. She remarked: 'You could put that tooth under

9

your pillow tonight, Timmy, and by morning the fairies might have left some money in its place.'

'I don't believe in fairies,' said Timmy.

'Very likely,' said his grandmother. 'But take care of that tooth anyway. You never know . . .'

And she gave Timmy the gold foil from one of her birthday chocolates to wrap his tooth in. 'Go on wrapping that tooth,' she said. 'Wrap it up well.'

Timmy went home with his gold tooth in his pocket.

He asked his mother for some silver kitchen-foil to wrap it in. So now it was wrapped in a layer of gold and a layer of silver on top of that.

The next day Timmy took out his silver tooth – rather a big tooth now – and wrapped it in a large green leaf from the garden. So now the tooth was wrapped in a layer of gold, a layer of silver, and a layer of green. By now it was much larger, and not really tooth-shaped any more, it was ball-shaped.

The next day Timmy wrapped his tooth-ball in some red paper left over from Christmas. So now the tooth was wrapped in layers of gold and silver and green and red. The tooth-ball was getting bigger and bigger; but, oddly enough, it was not getting heavier.

Every day now Timmy added another layer

of wrapping to his tooth-ball: a layer of writing-paper, of brown paper, of computer paper. By now the tooth-ball was bigger than a tennis-ball, but much, much lighter.

One day Timmy was playing in the front garden with his tooth-ball, when it sailed over the fence into the road. A boy who was passing caught it, and brought it back to Timmy.

'It's a strange ball,' said the boy.

'It's a tooth-ball,' said Timmy, and he explained all about it.

The boy said: 'My name's Jim, and I live in the next street. I've an old grey sock at home which would go over your tooth-ball, if you'd like that.'

'My name's Timmy,' said Timmy; 'and I would.'

So they went together to Jim's house and wrapped the tooth-ball in a layer of grey sock.

From now on Timmy and Jim together added a new wrapping to the tooth-ball every day.

They wrapped it in kitchen-paper and news-paper and wallpaper. They wrapped it in a duster, they wrapped it in cotton-wool and a tea-towel and an old woolly hat.

They wrapped it in a table-cloth and a pillow-case and a sack.

It got bigger and bigger – and lighter and lighter, too, in a most surprising way. They had to wrap it in garden-netting so that Timmy could wind his fingers in it firmly, to stop the tooth-ball from bouncing away.

Timmy and Jim took the tooth-ball to the park with them. They were playing with it, when a breeze blew it high over a clump of bushes and out of sight.

Timmy and Jim rushed round the bushes and came upon a whole gang of children who had been playing together. Now they were just standing and staring at the tooth-ball, which sat on the ground in the middle of them, looking interesting.

'Whatever is it?' asked a girl.

And a boy said: 'It's a huge raggedy balloon.'

'No,' said Timmy. 'It's a tooth-ball.' And he told them all the layers of wrapping; and Jim helped him to remember them in the right order.

Then they all began to play with the tooth-ball, batting it to and fro with their hands. By now the breeze had strengthened into a wind, which caught the tooth-ball and began to carry it up and away.

'Oh!' shrieked Timmy; and he caught the tooth-ball by a dangling end of netting as it was sailing past. But, instead of Timmy pulling the tooth-ball down to earth, the tooth-ball lifted Timmy skyward.

'Hold on to him someone!' shouted Jim; and someone – a boy called Ginger – did. But

the tooth-ball was carrying both of them upwards; so a girl caught hold of Ginger's ankles. Still they went up, all three of them. Then a boy caught the girl's feet, in the nick of time. Then a girl caught hold of him. Then another boy. Lastly, Jim.

The tooth-ball carried them all up and away, a trail of children in the sky.

They were blown on and on.

At last the wind died and they floated gently into a back garden that Timmy knew well. His grandmother came out of the house to greet them: 'Timmy, how nice that you've dropped in! And all your friends, too! I'll get tea.'

When she came back with the lemonade and the chocolate biscuits and the crisps, she found Timmy and all the others staring dolefully at the tooth-ball. 'It's gone dead,' said Timmy. 'Heavy.'

'We must find out what's wrong,' said Timmy's grandmother. 'We'll have to unwrap it.'

They took off the netting and the sack and the pillow-case and the table-cloth and the woolly hat and the tea-towel and the duster and the cotton-wool and the wallpaper and the newspaper and the kitchen-paper and the grey sock and the computer paper and the brown paper and the writing-paper and the red paper and green leaf and the silver foil – they took off all the layers of wrapping until, at the very centre of the ball, they came to the gold foil that Timmy had wrapped his tooth in, first of all.

But the gold foil was just a flat little bit of wrapping: there was no tooth inside it now.

'I was afraid of that,' said Timmy's grandmother. 'That tooth just wore itself out and *went*.'

'But a tooth doesn't do that,' said Timmy.

'A magic tooth does,' said his grandmother. 'This proves it.'

So, after tea, Timmy and his friends had to go home in the ordinary way, by bus.

Timmy was never able to make another tooth-ball; but he didn't mind too much. He had lots of friends instead.

And that's the end of the story.

St Pancras and King's Cross

Donald Bisset

Once upon a time there were two railway stations who lived right next door to each other. One was called St Pancras and the other King's Cross. They were always quarrelling as to which was the better station.

'I have diesel engines as well as steam engines at my station,' said St Pancras.

'Humph! So have I!' said King's Cross.

'And I've got a cafeteria,' said St Pancras.

'So have I!'

'Open on Sundays?'

'Yes, open on Sundays!'

'Humph!'

There was silence for a few minutes, then King's Cross said, 'Well, I've got ten platforms and you've only got seven.'

'I'm twice as tall as you are!' replied St Pancras. 'And, anyway, your clock is slow.'

The King's Cross clock was furious and ticked away as fast as it could to catch up. It ticked so fast that soon the St Pancras clock was away behind, and it ticked as fast as it could too, so as not to be out-done. They both got faster and faster; and the trains had to go faster too so as not to be late.

Quicker and quicker went the clocks and faster and faster went the trains, till at last they had no time even to set down their passengers, but started back again as soon as they had entered the station. The passengers were furious and waved their umbrellas out of the windows.

'Hi, stop!' they called. But the engines wouldn't.

'No!' they said. 'We can't stop or we'll be late. Can't you see the time?'

By now the clocks were going so fast that almost as soon as it was morning it was evening again.

The sun was very surprised. 'I must be going too slow!' it thought. So it hurried up and set almost as soon as it had risen and then rose again. The people all over London were in such a state getting up and going to bed, and then getting up again with hardly any sleep at all – and running to work so as not to be late, and the children running to school and hardly having time to say twice two are four and running home again.

Finally the Lord Mayor of London said to the Queen, 'Your Majesty, this won't do! I think we ought to go and give a medal to Euston Station, then the other two will be so jealous they may stop quarrelling.'

'That's a good idea!' said the Queen. So she set out from Buckingham Palace with the Lord Mayor and the Horse Guards and the Massed

Bands of the Brigade of Guards, and in front of her walked the Prime Minister carrying a gold medal on a red velvet cushion.

When they got to King's Cross the two stations stopped quarrelling and looked at them.

'Do you see what I see, St Pancras?' asked King's Cross.

'I do indeed!' said St Pancras. 'A medal being taken to Euston Station, just because it's got fifteen platforms. It's not fair! Why, you're a better station than Euston!'

'And so are you, St Pancras,' said King's Cross.

St Pancras was surprised, but it thought it would be nice to be friends after all the quarrelling, so it said, 'Let's be friends.'

'Yes, let's!' said King's Cross.

So they became friends and stopped quarrelling, and their clocks stopped going too fast and their trains stopped having to hurry. Everyone was very pleased.

'You are clever, Lord Mayor!' said the Queen.

'Thank you, Your Majesty,' said the Lord Mayor.

Harry and Amanda

Adèle Geras

Harry was making a list of all the reasons he could think of for being miserable. He ticked off each item on his fingers:

1) Being in hospital.
2) Having your tonsils out.
3) Having a sore throat.
4) Not being able to eat anything except ice-cream.

Harry paused. He'd almost run out of fingers on one hand already. Perhaps all those were really only one big misery called 'Having to Have Your Tonsils Out'. Apart from that, there was having to miss the Swimming Gala. Harry was the best swimmer in Otter Street Primary, and he'd been looking forward to the Gala for weeks.

'Why do I have to have my tonsils out this week?' he'd moaned at his mum. 'I haven't even got a sore throat at the moment.'

'Because now is when there's a space for you, so let's have no more of that whining!' Harry's mum had said.

The most miserable misery of all was the fact that sitting up in a bed almost opposite

Harry's in the ward was Amanda Goodbody. Harry's private name for her was 'Snobby Amanda', and she was the one person in his class who really annoyed him. She always wore clean white socks and polished black shoes, and her hair was always braided into lots and lots of little plaits. On special occasions, she tied ribbons on the ends of her plaits, and the bows looked like butterflies that had settled on her hair. She always got her sums right, and had the best writing in the class. Harry had some difficulty in making his letters join up smoothly and lie straight on top of the ruled lines on the paper. Amanda's letters behaved themselves beautifully and went exactly where she wanted them to go.

'There are some people,' Mrs Hughes would say, as she stapled another of Amanda's poems to the display board, 'who should take a leaf out of Amanda's book.' Then she would frown at Harry, whose page was full of blotches and thin patches where he'd been a bit energetic with his rubber. The main thing that annoyed Harry about Amanda, though, was the fact that she didn't seem to find him funny. Whenever he was cheeky to Mrs Hughes or naughty in class, all the other children giggled behind their fingers. Amanda always seemed to be looking the other way, or lining up the pencils in her pencil box, or just staring out of the window with her nose in the air.

Now here she was in the same ward, only three beds up from the one opposite Harry. She didn't look as stuck-up as she did at school, that was true. She was wearing blue pyjamas with flowers on them, and all her plaits were flat against her head. She looked much smaller than she did at school, too.

'Isn't it simply the most amazing coincidence?' Sister trilled after his operation, her big, square, white teeth flashing at him as she smiled. 'Two children from the same class in at the very same time for the very same operation! I've never known it to happen before, not in all my years of nursing.'

Harry mumbled something that he hoped sounded polite, but Sister wasn't really listening.

'Later on,' she said, 'when you both feel a bit stronger, perhaps you can play Snakes and Ladders or something. We've got all sorts of lovely board-games on that table over there.' Harry nodded miserably and closed his eyes. Sister strode down the ward in her squeaky shoes, leaving him to go on with his list. It was very short.

1) Everything I thought of before.

2) Snobby Amanda only three beds away on the other side of the ward.

Just after lunch it was officially Visiting Time, although people could really come and visit whenever they liked, because it was a children's ward. Amanda pretended to be reading her book, and tried to look as though she were perfectly happy that no one had come to visit her. It isn't Mum's fault, Amanda said to herself. She'd explained it all carefully: how she could only come in the evening after work, and how she would stay ever such a long time then. Maybe, Amanda thought, she'll stay right up until I've gone to sleep. Still, I wish Dad lived with us instead of with his new family right across the world in Australia. It was true that he wrote to Amanda and she wrote back, and also that he sent her wonderful presents, but it wasn't the same thing at all as having a dad who could come and sit by your bed when your throat was sore.

Amanda stared so hard at the picture in her book that all the lines began to look blurred and smudgy. If only Horrible Harry wasn't in the bed almost opposite hers! He would tell everyone in Mrs Hughes' class how no one had come to visit Amanda except her mother, and that even she only came at teatime.

Amanda looked across at Horrible Harry and had to admit he looked a bit less horrible than usual. For one thing, he was quiet. At school, he was always charging down corridors, bounding over desks, waving his arms around, shouting, snorting, and bumping into people accidentally-on-purpose, especially, it seemed to Amanda, into her. Also, dressed in his striped pyjamas, he looked quite clean. At school, his fingers were grey, his face streaked with this and that from the playground, and he always had yesterday's school dinner in crusty bits all over his sweater. He never seemed to sit still long enough to do any work. He would leap up and down from his chair instead of doing his sums or his writing, so it wasn't surprising they were always so messy. Amanda was amazed at how fast he could run, or how well he could climb a rope or leap over the boxes in PE. Whenever she had to do anything like that, she could feel Harry thinking she was silly.

'Girls are useless,' he'd said once, very loudly. 'Can't do anything properly.' Mrs Hughes had told him off for saying it, but Amanda had known he meant her really, and not all girls. Mumtaz and Donna were just as good at sports as Harry was and everybody knew it.

She looked across at Harry's family. His mum (plump) and his dad (skinny) were on chairs next to the bed, and his two brothers, one of about ten, and another who looked almost grown-up, were lying all over the bed, even though visitors weren't really supposed to. For a split second, Amanda wished she belonged to a different family – a mother and a father who weren't divorced and two sisters . . . or even one would do – and then she felt bad about wishing such a thing, and two small tears slid out of the corners of her eyes and rolled down her cheeks. Amanda lifted her book up in front of her face, hoping Harry hadn't seen her crying.

'Now then, you two,' said Sister, 'I do think it's silly, both of you sitting here like statues when you could be having fun!' She was pushing Harry and Amanda along the ward to the table near the door. 'I want you to sit here for a bit and jolly well enjoy yourselves.' She

showed her teeth. 'There's all sorts of games
. . . I shall come back and see you later.' She
squeaked away and Harry and Amanda sat
down at the table facing one another. There
was a long silence. Then:

'What shall we play?' asked Amanda.

'Dunno,' said Harry.

'Scrabble? Snakes and Ladders? Ludo?'

'Don't care, really,' said Harry. 'You
choose.'

'Snakes and Ladders, then.' Amanda took
out the board and they began to play.

'I'm going home tomorrow,' Harry said
suddenly.

'So am I.'

'Is your throat sore?'

'Yes,' said Amanda.

'Why didn't your mum and dad come and see you?'

Amanda looked down. 'Mum's got a job. She's coming at tea-time.'

'What about your dad?'

'He's in Australia. He's divorced from my mum.'

'My dad's cousin went to Australia,' said Harry. 'We get cards from him sometimes. One of them had a koala bear on it.'

'I love koalas. I'll write to my dad and maybe he'll send me one.'

'He can't send a real bear,' said Harry. 'It's not allowed.'

'Not a real one, silly. A postcard with a picture of one on it like the one you got.'

Harry looked at Amanda. She seemed to be quite normal. She seemed quite happy to chat.

'You're different in hospital,' Harry said.

'So are you.'

'You're not all snobby and goody-goody.'

'And you're not all noisy and dirty.'

'I call you "Snobby Amanda" at school.'

'I call you "Horrible Harry".'

'But I'm not horrible,' Harry said. 'Am I?'

'Not in here,' said Amanda. 'I'm not snobby, either.'

'No, you're not,' Harry agreed. 'Not in here.'

'Let's get on with the game.'

Harry and Amanda played Snakes and Ladders, then they played Ludo, then they watched television in the day-room. At Visiting Time, when Amanda's mum came to see her, she said: 'Isn't that the boy you're always going on about . . . that Harry somebody. Don't you call him "Horrible Harry"?'

'He's nice really,' said Amanda, 'when you get to know him. I'm teaching him how to play Junior Scrabble after you've gone.'

Harry's mum said: 'Who's that you're waving to, then?'

'It's someone from my class,' said Harry. 'She's called Amanda. She's going to teach me how to play Junior Scrabble when you've all gone home.'

Harry's brothers started giggling and prodding each other.

'Harry's got a girlfriend! Harry's got a girlfriend!' they chanted.

'We're friends,' said Harry. 'That's all. So why don't you both shut up?'

Copycat

Irene Rawnsley

Every time we have painting
Jonathan copies me.

Today I did a red house
with a chimney on top,
made smoke come out,
put curtains at the window,
a cat on the doorstep,
a tree in the garden
with one blackbird,
a path, a gate,
and a big sun shining.

When I looked at his picture
Jonathan had copied me.

He had a red house,
a smoking chimney,
a cat on the doorstep,
curtains at the window,
a garden, a tree
with a blackbird perched
on the same branch,
a path leading to a gate
and a big sun shining.

The teacher said, 'Which of you copied?'
But I didn't tell.
Jonathan's a copycat
but he's my friend as well.

Gloria Who Might Be
My Best Friend

Ann Cameron

If you have a girl for a friend, people find
out and tease you. That's why I didn't want
a girl for a friend – not until this summer,
when I met Gloria.

It happened one afternoon when I was
walking down the street by myself. My
mother was visiting a friend of hers, and Huey
was visiting a friend of his. Huey's friend is
five and so I think he is too young to play
with. And there aren't any kids just my age.
I was walking down the street feeling lonely.

Near our house I saw a moving van in front
of a brown house, and men were carrying in
chairs and tables and bookcases and boxes full
of I don't know what. I watched for a while,
and suddenly I heard a voice right behind me.

'Who are you?'

I turned around and there was a girl in a
yellow dress. She looked the same age as me.
She had curly hair that was braided into two
pigtails with red ribbons at the ends.

'I'm Julian,' I said. 'Who are you?'

'I'm Gloria,' she said. 'I come from New-port. Do you know where Newport is?'

I wasn't sure, but I didn't tell Gloria. 'It's a town by the sea,' I said.

'Right,' Gloria said. 'Can you turn a cart-wheel?'

She turned sideways herself and did two cartwheels on the grass.

I had never tried a cartwheel before, but I tried to copy Gloria. My hands went down in the grass, my feet went up in the air, and – I fell over.

I looked at Gloria to see if she was laughing at me. If she was laughing at me, I was going to go home and forget about her.

But she just looked at me very seriously and said, 'It takes practice,' and then I liked her.

'I know where there's a bird's nest in your garden,' I said.

'Really?' Gloria said. 'There weren't any trees in the garden, or any birds, where I lived before.'

I showed her where a robin nests and has eggs. Gloria stood up on a branch and looked in. The eggs were small and white. The mother robin squawked at us, and she and the father robin flew around our heads.

'They want us to go away,' Gloria said. She got down from the branch, and we went around to the front of the house and watched the moving men carry two rugs and a mirror inside.

'Would you like to come over to my house?'
I said.

'All right,' Gloria said, 'if it is all right with
my mother.' She ran in the house and asked.

It was all right, so Gloria and I went to
my house, and I showed her my room and
my games and my rock collection, and then
I made strawberry soda and we sat at the kitchen table and drank it.

'You have a red moustache on your mouth,'
Gloria said.

'You have a red moustache on your mouth,
too,' I said.

Gloria giggled, and we licked off the mous-
taches with our tongues.

'I wish you'd live here a long time,' I told
Gloria.

Gloria said, 'I wish I would too.'

'I know the best way to make wishes,'
Gloria said.

'What's that?' I asked.

'First you make a kite. Do you know how
to make one?'

'Yes,' I said, 'I know how.' I know how
to make good kites because my father taught
me. We make them out of two crossed sticks
and folded newspaper.

'All right,' Gloria said, 'that's the first part
of making wishes that come true. So let's make
a kite.'

We went out into the garage and spread

out sticks and newspaper and made a kite. I fastened on the kite string and went to the cupboard and got rags for the tail.

'Do you have some paper and two pencils?' Gloria asked. 'Because now we make the wishes.'

I didn't know what she was planning, but I went in the house and got pencils and paper.

'All right,' Gloria said, 'Every wish you want to have come true you write on a long thin piece of paper. You don't tell me your wishes, and I don't tell you mine. If you tell, your wishes don't come true. Also, if you look at the other person's wishes, your wishes don't come true.'

Gloria sat down on the garage floor again and started writing her wishes. I wanted to see what they were – but I went to the other side of the garage and wrote my own wishes instead. I wrote:

1. I wish the fig tree would be the tallest in town.
2. I wish I'd be a great football player.
3. I wish I could ride in an aeroplane
4. I wish Gloria would stay here and be my best friend.

I folded my four wishes in my fist and went over to Gloria.

33

'How many wishes did you make?' Gloria asked.

'Four,' I said. 'How many did you make?'

'Two,' Gloria said.

I wondered what they were.

'Now we put the wishes on the tail of the kite,' Gloria said. 'Every time we tie one piece of rag on the tail, we fasten a wish in the knot. You can put yours in first.'

I fastened mine in, and then Gloria fastened in hers, and we carried the kite into the yard.

'You hold the tail,' I told Gloria, 'and I'll pull.'

We ran through the back yard with the kite, passed the garden and the fig tree, and went into the open field beyond our garden.

The kite started to rise. The tail jerked heavily like a long white snake. In a minute the kite passed the roof of my house and was climbing towards the sun.

We stood in the open field, looking up at it. I was wishing I would get my wishes.

'I know it's going to work!' Gloria said.

'How do you know?'

'When we take the kite down,' Gloria told me, 'there shouldn't be one wish in the tail. When the wind takes all your wishes, that's when you know it's going to work.'

The kite stayed up for a long time. We both held the string. The kite looked like a tiny black spot in the sun, and my neck got stiff from looking at it.

'Shall we pull it in?' I asked.

'All right,' Gloria said.

We drew the string in more and more until, like a tired bird, the kite fell at our feet.

We looked at the tail. All our wishes were gone. Probably they were still flying higher and higher in the wind.

Maybe I would get to be a good football player and have a ride in an aeroplane and have the tallest fig tree in town. And Gloria would be my best friend.

'Gloria,' I said, 'did you wish we would be friends?'

'You're not supposed to ask me that!' Gloria said.

'I'm sorry,' I answered. But inside I was smiling. I guessed one thing Gloria wished for. I was pretty sure we would be friends.

Nittle and Bubberlink

Richard Edwards

Quick was the Bubberlink, speedy was she,
Lived all alone in the fork of a tree,
Charged through the undergrowth, hurtled
and leapt,
Raced through the forest while other things
slept.

Slow was the Nittle and plodding and round,
Lived all alone in a hole in the ground,
Sauntered through barley fields, strolled in the
corn,
Dawdled and dithered from dusk until dawn.

Sad was the Bubberlink, cheerless was she,
Sad was the Nittle, as glum as could be;
Each friendless evening they'd rise from their
      beds
Weeping a little and shaking their heads;

Till one warm night in the middle of June
As they roamed out by the light of the moon,
Suddenly crossing the same mothy space –
Nittle and Bubberlink came face to face.

Now, not too quickly, but neither too slow,
Down the dark lanes of the woodland they
      go:
Nittle and Bubberlink, hand in hand, friends,
Walking together until the world ends.

The Boy in the Garden

Berlie Doherty

Andrew lives in a big house on the top of a
hill. The stairs creak when he goes up them.
When he talks, his voice bounces back to him.
There are so many rooms that he can't count
them all. He has to go right back to the begin-
ning and start again, and before he gets to the
end he's forgotten. His bedroom is at the very
top of the house, and from his window he
can see the lights of the town twinkling like
yellow stars, far away.

'Please can we go back and live in our old
house?' he asks his mum every night when
she puts him to bed.

She laughs and kisses him. 'But this is a
wonderful house,' she says. 'Don't you like
it?'

'No,' Andrew says.

One day she told him why they had bought
such a big house. 'We're going to use it as
a home for old people,' she told him. 'They'll
be coming to live with us soon. That will be
nice, won't it?'

'It won't be nice for me,' said Andrew. 'I'm
not old. I'm only a little boy.'

'Oh dear,' his mum sighed. 'I wish you liked it here. It's got a lovely garden, hasn't it?'

'I don't like gardens.' Andrew turned away from his mother. In his last garden he had made a tunnel in the hedge for the children next door to crawl through. He felt like crying. 'There's no one to play with here.'

'Don't you worry,' his mother said. 'You'll soon make friends.'

One night when Andrew couldn't get to sleep he thought he could hear the sound of someone running in the garden. He sat up in bed. He could. He could hear laughter, he was sure. He crept over the creaking floorboards

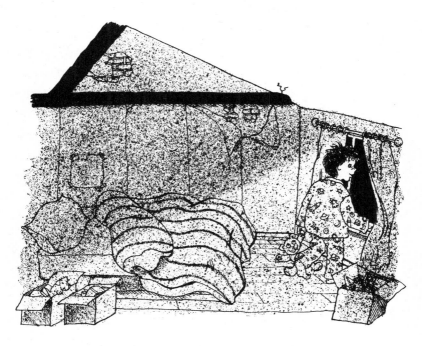

and looked out of his window. It was a bright moonlight night. The long grass in the garden was deep in the shadow of the house, but someone was there, he was sure of it. A boy was down there, looking up at him, holding something up in his hand. As soon as he saw Andrew, he put the something down in the grass and ran off. There it was, far below him, something small and round waiting for him.

It was a ball. Andrew picked it up the next morning and ran upstairs to his room with it. It was so small that he could nearly close it inside the fingers of his two hands to hide it. It was striped with wavy colours – red, blue, yellow, green, white – and the colours were old, as if they had been in the sunshine a long time. Andrew loved it. He bounced it on the floor and it zig-zagged away from him. He dived under his bed to find it and it bounced up the other side against the wardrobe. Wherever he jumped, it bounced the other way. His mum heard him laughing and thumping as he ran round the room after it, and she came in to see what all the noise was about.

'I'm having fun!' said Andrew. 'Catch!' He bounced it towards her and as she put out her hands, it bobbed away round the room and into one of Andrew's shoes.

'Go and have fun with it in the garden,' she laughed. 'The decorators are coming today, so we need you out of the way. Weren't you lucky to find that ball!'

He clattered down the stairs, the ball tight in his hand. He hadn't found it. He knew that. It was a present.

He played with it all day. Sometimes it seemed as if the ball would never stop bouncing. When it was nearly dark, his mum called him in to tea and he gave it one last bounce. He chased it into a bush and it bounced right up again from the other side. Andrew scrambled out of the bush and stared after it. It couldn't have done that on its own, surely. Someone must be throwing it.

'Are you there?' he shouted into the bushes. 'Boy? Are you there?' He could hear the rustle of twigs and the light pealing of laughter. It could have been a hedgehog scurrying through the bushes. It could have been a bird singing in the trees. But he knew it wasn't.

'You are there, aren't you?' he whispered.

And then he realised that he had lost his ball. It was nearly dark, and his mum was calling him, and he couldn't find his ball.

'When I call you, you come in, do you hear me?' His mum took his hand to lead him back into the house.

'But I've lost my ball, Mum,' he wailed. He twisted round to look over his shoulder, sure that he would see his stripy ball gleaming in the grass. But it wasn't there.

'You'll find it in the morning,' his mum said. 'Come and see how lovely the house looks. The decorators have finished.'

But Andrew wasn't interested in the new wallpaper. All he wanted was his ball.

'The first of the guests will be coming on Saturday,' his mum told him. 'That's exciting, isn't it?'

'No,' said Andrew. He would have to be quiet in case he woke the old people up when they were dozing. He would have to walk slowly in case he knocked them over. He would have to pick up all his toys in case they tripped over them. Anyway, he didn't want his toys any more. He wanted his ball.

'And you'll be starting school on Monday, so there'll be lots of friends for you,' said his dad. 'You'll be all right.'

But Andrew didn't want lots of friends. He wanted the boy in the garden. He wanted to see him.

That night he crouched on his windowsill and watched the garden growing really dark. He could hardly keep his eyes open. He heard his mum and dad going to bed and still he watched. He was just about to give up and climb into bed, when he heard it again: the sound of someone running, and the sound of someone laughing. And there he was again, just there in the shadows, hardly there at all really – a boy, holding up the stripy ball, and putting it down in the grass.

Andrew rushed down to get the ball as soon as it was morning. He skipped into the house with it and bounced it round the kitchen, and then he ran upstairs, throwing it up in front of him and catching it as it lollopped back. He bounced it into his room.

'Outside with that!' his mum shouted. 'The carpets are coming today.'

Andrew leaned out of his window and dropped the ball down. It bounced back up again, nearly as high, and again, and again, till the bounces grew lower and lower and stopped altogether. It rolled under a bush. A second later, it bounced up high again. Yes! The boy must be there again. Andrew ran outside and spent the whole day throwing and catching and bouncing with the boy he couldn't see.

On Saturday the first of the old people was moving in. It was a gentleman called Mr Toby. Dad was going to meet him from the station, and Mum thought it was a good idea if Andrew went too. 'We want Mr Toby to feel at home,' she said. 'It was his home when he was a little boy. He used to live here. It will be really nice for him if you go to meet him at the station.'

Andrew didn't want to go. He dropped the ball out of his window and watched the bounces growing lower and lower. At least the boy could play with it while he was out.

Mr Toby had a round, red face. He talked all the way back from the station and Andrew sat in the back of the car and stared at him. He liked him. He couldn't help it. Every time Mr Toby smiled at him, he just had to smile back. 'You can call me Toby, young lad,' whispered Mr Toby. 'But nobody else can.'

When they drove up to the house Mr Toby leaned back in his seat and sighed.

'Are you going to cry, Toby?' Andrew asked him.

'No,' said Mr Toby. 'Of course I'm not.' His eyes were shining. 'When I was a little chap like you, I used to live here.'

Mum showed Mr Toby his room. Andrew ran round the garden looking for his ball, and put it safe in his pocket. Maybe he would show it to Mr Toby later on.

'Andrew,' his mum called. 'I've made Mr Toby a nice cup of tea. Would you be a very careful boy and carry it in for him?'

Andrew carried the cup and saucer in without spilling a drop. He stuck his tongue between his teeth so he wouldn't breathe too hard. Mr Toby was dozing in a chair by the window, snoring a bit, but as soon as Andrew put the cup down he opened his eyes and winked at him.

'Caught me at it!' he chuckled. 'I'm always dozing, Andrew. Are you?'

44

'Sometimes,' said Andrew.

Mr Toby picked up the cup and sucked noisily at his tea. 'What do you dream about when you're dozing?'

'Ghosts,' said Andrew.

'I don't,' said Mr Toby. 'I dream about being a little boy. Old people do, you know. I dream I'm a little boy again, playing in this garden here. Playing with my ball.'

'With your ball?' said Andrew.

'I used to have a little stripy ball that bounced and bounced and bounced,' said Mr Toby. He sucked his tea again. 'I loved that ball. And one day I put it somewhere safe, and I never found it again.' He put down his cup and closed his eyes. 'Every time I go to sleep, I dream I'm playing in the garden with it.'

'I think I've seen you,' said Andrew, but in a very small voice. He put his hand in his pocket. The ball felt warm and smooth. He rolled it from one hand to the other then let it drop on the floor. It bounced across the new carpet with a pattering sound. Mr Toby opened his eyes at once.

'That's it!' he said. 'That's my stripy ball!'

'I know,' said Andrew. He picked it up and handed it to Mr Toby. His throat was hurting a bit.

Mr Toby cupped it in his hand. 'Let's take it outside,' he said. 'Or your mum will shout at us.'

'Where are you two off to?' Andrew's mum said when she passed them in the corridor.

'I'm going to play out with Toby,' said Andrew.

Mr Toby put a hand on Andrew's shoulder, because he wasn't very steady on his feet, and proudly Andrew helped him down the step into the garden. Mr Toby took a deep breath and held up the ball.

'You can do the running, and I'll do the throwing, and the ball can do the bouncing,' he said. 'Ready?'

'Ready!' said Andrew.

And up went the ball, higher and higher and higher, bounce bounce bounce, all over Andrew and Toby's garden.

Littlenose Meets Two-Eyes

John Grant

Littlenose was a boy who lived long, long ago. His people were called the Neanderthal folk. In the days when they lived, the world was very cold. It was called the Ice Age.

There were lots of wild animals. Lions, tigers, bears and wolves had thick furry coats to keep them warm. Even the rhinoceros, and a kind of elephant called a mammoth, were big woolly creatures.

The Neanderthal folk were stocky, sturdy people with short necks and big noses. They were very proud of their noses, which were large and snuffly. Littlenose got his name because his nose was no bigger than a berry.

Littlenose's home was not a house, but a cave where he lived with his father and mother. Near the front of the cave a huge fire was always burning. This kept the family warm, and also frightened away wild crea-

tures, which was just as well because there was no door on the cave.

Sometimes Littlenose was naughty, and that could be dangerous. A child who strayed from his family cave, or loitered on an errand, might be eaten by a sabre-tooth tiger, or squashed flats as a pancake by a woolly rhinoceros.

But today Littlenose had been very naughty indeed. While his parents were hunting, he had let the fire go out.

Now he sat at the back of the cave and watched Father trying to re-light it. Father had two stones called flints which he banged together to make a spark. (There were no matches in those days.) But he couldn't strike a spark.

'Perhaps you need a new flint,' said Mother.

'I'll need a new son if he lets the fire out again,' grumbled Father. Littlenose expected to be thrown to the bears right away.

However, as they had no fire, Father blocked the cave entrance with rocks to keep out wild beasts. In the morning they had a cold breakfast. Father got ready to go for the flint.

'Have you enough money?' said Mother.

'I think so,' said Father, and pulled out a handful of the coloured pebbles which they used for money.

He kissed Mother goodbye, and was just going when Littlenose said, 'Can I come too?'

For a moment Father said nothing. Then: 'After the way you behaved, yesterday?' he exclaimed. 'Oh, all right,' and off he went, leaving Littlenose to follow.

'Goodbye, Littlenose,' Mother called after him. 'Be good. And always look both ways before you cross.'

But Littlenose wasn't listening. He was thinking about his secret. He had a pebble of his own. A green pebble, which he had found by the river. He had never been to a market before. But he was sure he would see something worth buying today.

They made their way by a woodland path. Father strode along with his club in his hand, and Littlenose skipped gaily behind him. Ahead, the path was crossed by a broad animal trail. Littlenose was about to dash straight across, when a cuff on the ear nearly knocked him down.

'Don't you *ever* do what Mother tells you?' said Father, angrily. Shamefaced, Littlenose stood on the grass verge and:

> Looked right!
> Looked left!
> And right again!

As he looked right the second time, a herd of woolly rhinoceros came round the bend. He and father dived into the bushes. They lay hidden as the great beasts lumbered by. Their small eyes blinked through their fur, and their long horns looked very dangerous.

When the rhinos had passed, Littlenose and Father went on their way.

Littlenose felt he had been walking for ever. But soon they left the woods and began climbing a grassy hillside. At last they came to a circle of trees. Littlenose realised that this was the market.

There seemed to be hundreds of people. Littlenose hadn't thought there were so many people in the whole world. He trotted behind Father, and he was bumped, pushed, trodden on, tripped over and shouted at. The sheer noise made him speechless – but not for long.

Suddenly: 'I'm hungry,' he said.

'You're always hungry,' grumbled Father. But he bought each of them a steaming hot hunk of meat from a man who was roasting a deer over a fire.

Then he went over to an old man who was sitting under a tree. There was a sign with his name on it.

At least, Littlenose thought it was his name. When he got closer, he saw that it had once read:

But the words were faded with the weather. Only 'Skin' and 'Flint' could be made out now. Most people thought it was the old man's name.

Neither Father nor the old man seemed in a hurry to settle about the new flint. Littlenose soon grew bored.

He wandered through the market, looking here and listening there. Everyone was bustling about buying the things they couldn't find or make for themselves. There were bone and ivory combs, and needles and pins. There were strange nuts, fruits and berries. And there were furs. Hundreds and hundreds of furs. From tiny mink and ermine to enormous white bear skins from the far north.

But Littlenose didn't see anything he wanted to buy. He had almost decided to keep his pebble for another day, when, over the heads of the crowd, he saw a sign.

Littlenose pushed forward. In a clear space, a little man stood on a tree stump.

'Five red pebbles I'm bid,' he shouted. 'Five! Going at five! Going! Going! GONE!

Sold to the gentleman in the lion-skin for five red pebbles.'

The gentleman in the lion-skin counted out his money. Then a huge woolly mammoth was led over to him.

'Oh,' thought Littlenose, 'if only I could buy one of those. I would march home, leading him by his trunk. Everyone would cheer. When I got home I would . . . oh, dear no! I forgot. I'm not even allowed pet mice in the cave. Anyway, a mammoth would hardly get its tail through the door. And that's about all I could buy with my pebble.'

And, feeling very said, Littlenose walked away. He sat down by the mammoth pen to rest. The pen was built of huge logs and was too high to see over.

Suddenly he jumped. Something soft and warm had tickled his neck.

It was a trunk – a very little one.

Littlenose looked through the bars of the pen. He saw the smallest, woolliest, saddest mammoth you could imagine. He climbed up and reached over the top rail to stroke its furry ears.

Suddenly he was seized by the scruff of his neck. A voice said: 'And what are you doing, young man?'

It was the man who owned the mammoths.

'Please,' said Littlenose, 'I was just looking at the mammoth.'

'Don't tell stories,' said the man. 'We've sold them all.'

But at that moment the trunk came through the bars again. It tickled the man's leg and he dropped Littlenose.

'They've done it again,' the man shouted to his assistant, who came running. 'Slipped in a reject! It's much too small to sell. And look, the eyes don't match! One's red and one's green. Who's going to buy this sort of animal?'

'I will,' said Littlenose, holding out his pebble.

Looking very relieved the man said: 'Well, I can't charge you more than eight white pebbles for a reject.' He took the green pebble from Littlenose, and gave him two white ones as change. The assistant opened the pen, and the little mammoth trotted out.

'One red eye and one green eye,' said Littlenose. 'That makes two eyes. I shall call you that. Come along, Two-Eyes.'

Littlenose stopped and bought a bundle of bone needles for Mother with his last two pebbles. The market was almost deserted now.

He started looking for Father, but Father found him first.

'Where *have* you been?' he shouted.

'Do you like my mammoth?' asked Littlenose.

'Mammoth? MAMMOTH?' roared Father. 'Are you playing with other people's property? Take it back where you found it. No, wait, we haven't time.' He waved his arms in the air, and gave a loud yell. Two-Eyes went scampering away into the trees.

'But he's mine. I *bought* him,' wailed Littlenose.

But Father wasn't listening – he was already striding away down the hillside. Littlenose hurried after him. The evening mist began to close in, and the sun became a dull red ball low in the sky.

'Don't dawdle, you'll get lost,' called out Father. But Littlenose kept tripping in the long grass. Each time he looked up it was darker, and even harder to see his father.

He ran on, stumbling and tripping.

Then he fell!

When he got up again, he was alone. 'Father!' he called. 'FATHER!' But all he heard was the echo of his own voice.

He began to run. He had never been lost before, and he was very frightened. All sorts of terrible things might be waiting in the mist to jump out at him. As he ran, the sun set. It became pitch dark . . .

All around him he could hear animals growling and snorting. They rustled in the undergrowth, and brushed past him as he ran. He stopped to catch his breath. There was a sound behind him. It was growing louder.

Littlenose began to run again. But, as fast

as he ran, the noise came closer. Suddenly he tripped again and fell.

Too frightened to move, Littlenose lay with his eyes closed. The sound grew louder. He could hear an animal breathing, but he dared not look up.

At the cave, Mother looked out as darkness fell. There was a sound of footsteps, and Father groped his way in.

'Where's Littlenose?' asked Mother.

'Isn't he here?' said Father. 'I thought the young rascal must have hurried home ahead of me.'

'Oh,' said Mother, 'he must be lost out there in the dark. You must find him!'

Quickly, Father lit the fire, took a branch for a torch, and turned back the way he had come.

The mist had gone and the moon was shining. The path lay clear before him. There were animal sounds among the trees. But there was no sign of Littlenose.

Then something moved towards him. Father's torch glinted on a pair of eyes. One red eye. One green eye. It was a small mammoth, and sitting on its back was Littlenose.

'Hello, Father,' he said. 'I got lost, and Two-Eyes followed me and brought me home.'

Mother saw the strange procession approaching the cave. Father was leading Two-Eyes by the trunk. Littlenose, his head nodding, sat on the mammoth's back.

A few moments later, Mother was tucking Littlenose in bed. He held out a little bundle. 'I bought you some needles at the market,' he said, and fell asleep.

The little mammoth was patiently waiting outside. Father took its trunk gently in his hand. He led it past the fire and into the corner where Littlenose slept. With a contented sigh and looking for all the world like an enormous ball of wool, Two-Eyes fell asleep as well.

Mr Greentoe's Crocodile

Jean Kenward

Mr Greentoe had a garden shed. There were all sorts of things in it: flower pots and string, a lawn mower, a mouse's nest, and some blue tits who had settled in the roof. There was a wheelbarrow, too. It had a red handle, and yellow legs.

Mr Greentoe loved his wheelbarrow.

Sometimes he filled it with leaf mould. Sometimes he filled it with firewood. Sometimes he had a good clear out and filled it with odds and ends that were not wanted any more.

Then Mr Greentoe trundled off to the tip.

One day, Mr Greentoe wanted to take a great load of rubbish to the tip in his barrow.

'I'm just off,' he called to his wife. 'Have you any rubbish for me to take?'

'You can take my old hoover,' she said to him. 'I don't want it any more.'

Mr Greentoe put the hoover on top of everything else. He put three cups with no handles on top of the hoover. He put a broken bread-bin on top of the cups.

He set off for the dump.

People called out to him as he went by.

'Will you take something to the tip for me, please, Mr Greentoe?' they shouted.

'Yes, I will!'

Mr Greentoe always said yes.

Soon his wheelbarrow was piled so high he could hardly see over the top.

When he got to the dump, he emptied it out.

My word! What a great heap of rubbish! Whew!

But something was moving among the rubbish. Something with a long tail . . . and a long snout . . . and claws . . . and teeth . . .

'Help! It's a crocodile!' gasped Mr Greentoe. 'Someone has thrown a crocodile out with the junk!'

He ran. The crocodile ran after him.

Mr Greentoe ran over the rubbish dump as fast as he could. He found an old oven with a broken door. The door was loose.

He crept inside . . .

Was he safe? Or wasn't he?

Mr Greentoe wasn't sure.

Soon the crocodile came up, panting.

'You needn't run so fast,' he told him. 'I shan't eat you. I'm a kindly crocodile. Look, I can smile!'

The crocodile opened his mouth very wide. Mr Greentoe could see his back teeth.

'I don't think I'll come out of the oven just yet,' said Mr Greentoe. He felt faint.

The crocodile was sad. 'No one likes me,' he wept. Tears ran down his nose.

Mr Greentoe was touched. 'Don't cry,' he said, taking a closer look at the crocodile. 'Why! You are a home-made crocodile,' he told him happily. 'I can see the stitches in your tail. I can see the stuffing in your tummy – there's a hole there. Some of it is coming out.'

'That's why they threw me away,' explained the crocodile. 'No one wants me any more. Not with a hole.'

'I do!'

Mr Greentoe came out of the oven. He shut the broken door with a clang. 'You can come home with me,' he told the kindly crocodile. 'My wife will mend your tummy. Get in my wheelbarrow.'

The crocodile climbed into the wheelbarrow. Trundle bump, trundle bump ... Mr Greentoe wheeled him home.

'What have you got there?' asked his wife.

'I've got a kindly crocodile,' said Mr Green-toe. 'He's going to live in the garden shed. There's a tin bath outside that will do for a pond.'

'Goodness! You don't say!'

Mr Greentoe's wife was surprised. She found her sewing basket. She found her needle, and some strong thread. She sewed up the kindly crocodile's tummy, while he had forty winks. It didn't hurt.

Mr Greentoe made him a comfortable place in his shed. He poured water in the tin bath.

'You can stay here with the mice and blue tits,' he promised.

When people heard that Mr Greentoe had a crocodile in his shed, they all came to look.

Sometimes they saw him swimming.

Sometimes they took him for a ride in the wheelbarrow.

Sometimes they brought him sardines to eat. They knitted squares into a blanket for him. In winter, when snow fell and there was ice on the tin bath, Mr Greentoe wheeled his barrow into the kitchen, and the kindly croco-dile came in with it, under his blanket.

He didn't cry any more. His button eyes shone. He smiled with his back teeth.

He was happy.

My Party

Kit Wright

My parents said I could have a party
And that's just what I did.

Dad said, 'Who had you thought of inviting?'
I told him. He said, 'Well, you'd better start
    writing,'
And that's just what I did

To:
Phyllis Willis, Horace Morris,
Nancy, Clancy, Bert and Gert Sturt,
Dick and Mick and Nick Crick,
Ron, Don, John,
Dolly, Molly, Polly –
Neil Peel –
And my dear old friend, Dave Dirt.

I wrote, 'Come along, I'm having a party,'
And that's just what they did.

They all arrived with huge appetites
As Dad and I were fixing the lights.
I said, 'Help yourself to the drinks and bites!'
And that's just what they did,
All of them:

Phyllis Willis, Horace Morris,
Nancy, Clancy, Bert and Gert Sturt,
Dick and Mick and Nick Crick,
Ron, Don, John,
Dolly, Molly, Polly –
Neil Peel –
And my dear old friend, Dave Dirt.

Now, I had a good time and as far as I could
        tell,
The party seemed to go pretty well –
Yes, that's just what it did.

Then Dad said, 'Come on, just for fun,
Let's have a *turn* from everyone!'
And a turn's just what they did,

All of them: .

Phyllis Willis, Horace Morris,
Nancy, Clancy, Bert and Gert Sturt,
Dick and Mick and Nick Crick,
Ron, Don, John,
Dolly, Molly, Polly –
Neil Peel –
And my dear old friend, Dave Dirt.

AND THIS IS WHAT THEY DID:

Phyllis and Clancy
And Horace and Nancy
Did a song and dance number
That was really fancy –

Dolly, Molly, Polly,
Ron, Don and John
Performed a play
That went on and on and on –

Gert and Bert Sturt,
Sister and brother,
Did an imitation of
Each other.

(Gert Sturt put on Bert Sturt's shirt
And Bert Sturt put on Gert Sturt's skirt.)

Neil Peel
All on his own
Danced an eightsome reel.

Dick and Mick
And Nicholas Crick
Did a most *ingenious*
Conjuring trick

And my dear old friend, Dave Dirt,
Was terribly sick
All over the flowers.
We cleaned it up.
It took *hours*.

But as Dad said, giving a party's not easy.
You really
Have to
Stick at it.
I agree. And if Dave gives a party
I'm certainly
Going to be
Sick at it.

The story of Giant Kippernose

John Cunliffe

Once there was a giant called Kippernose. He lived on a lonely farm in the mountains. He was not fierce. Indeed he was as kind and gentle as a giant could be. He liked children, and was fond of animals. He was good at telling stories. His favourite foods were ice-cream, cakes, lollipops and sausages. He would help anyone, large or small. And yet he had no friends. When he went to the town to do his shopping, everyone ran away from him. Busy streets emptied in a trice. Everyone ran home, bolted their doors and closed all their windows, even on hot summer days.

Kippernose shouted, 'Don't run away! I'll not hurt you! Please don't run away, I like little people. I've only come to do my shopping. Please come out. I'll tell you a good story about a dragon and a mermaid.'

But it was no use. The town stayed silent and empty; the doors and windows stayed firmly closed. Poor Kippernose wanted so much to have someone to talk to. He felt so lonely that he often sat down in the town square and cried his heart out. You would think someone would take pity on him, but no one ever did. He simply could not understand it. He even tried going to another town, far across the mountains, but just the same thing happened.

'Has all the world gone mad?' said Kippernose to himself, and took his solitary way home.

The truth was that the people were not afraid of Kippernose, and they had not gone mad, either. The truth *was* . . . that Kippernose had not had a single bath in a hundred years or more! The poor fellow carried such a stink wherever he went that everyone with a nose on his face ran for cover at the first whiff. Oh, how that giant reeked! Pooh, you could smell him a mile away, and worst of all on hot days. People buried their noses in flowers and lavender-bags, but still the stench crept in. The wives cried shame and shame upon him, and swore that his stink turned their milk sour, and their butter rancid. What made matters worse, he never washed his hair or his whiskers, either. Smelly whiskers bristled all over his chin, and little creatures crept amongst them. His greasy hair fell down his back. He never used a comb. He never brushed his teeth. *And*, quite often, he went to bed with his boots on.

When he was a boy, Kippernose was always clean and smart, his mother saw to that. Long

long ago, his good mother had gone off to
live in far Cathay, and he had forgotten all
she had told him about keeping clean and tidy,
and changing his socks once a week. It was
a lucky thing when his socks wore out, because
that was the only time he would change them.
He had no notion of the sight and smell he
was. He never looked in a mirror. His smell
had grown up with him, and he didn't notice
it at all. His mind was deep among tales of
dragons and wizards, for people in stories were
his only friends. If only someone could have
told him about his smell, in a nice way, all
would have been well.

The people grumbled enough amongst themselves. Mrs Dobson, of Ivy Cottage, was one of them. Friday was market day, and ironing day too, and every Friday night she would bang her iron angrily, and say to quiet Mr Dobson by the fireside, 'That giant's a scandal. It's every market day we have the sickening stench of him, and the whole pantry turned sour and rotten, too. Can't you men do something about it? You sit there and warm your toes, and nod off to sleep, while the world's going to ruin . . .'

'But, Bessie, my dear,' mild Mr Dobson answered, 'what can we do? You cannot expect anyone to go up to an enormous giant and say – I say, old chap, you smell most dreadfully – now can you? Besides, no one could get near enough to him: the smell would drive them away.'

'You could send him a letter,' said Mrs Dobson.

'But he cannot read. He never went to school. Even as a boy, Kippernose was too big to get through the school door, my old grandfather used to say.'

'Well, the government should do something about it,' said Mrs Dobson, banging on. 'If that Queen of ours came out of her palace and took a sniff of our Kippernose, *she'd* do something quickly enough, I'll bet.'

But it was not the Queen, or the government, or Mr Dobson, who solved the problem in the end. It was a creature so small that no one could see it.

One Friday in the middle of winter, a cold day of ice and fog, Kippernose went to town to do his shopping as usual. He felt so unhappy that he didn't even bother to call out and ask the people to stay to talk to him. He just walked gloomily into the market-place.

'It's no good,' he said to himself, 'they'll never be friends with me. They don't seem to think a giant has feelings, like anyone else, I might just as well be . . .'

'Hoi! Look where you're going!' an angry voice shouted up from the foggy street. 'Oh, I say, oh, help!'

Then there was a great crash, and there were apples rolling everywhere. Then a babble of voices gathered round Kippernose.

'The clumsy great oaf – look he's knocked Jim Surtees' apple-cart over. Did you ever see such a mess? Tramping about, not looking where he's going, with his head in the sky.'

Amongst all this angry noise stood Kippernose, with an enormous smile spreading across his big face. The smile grew to a grin.

'*They're not running away*. They're *not running away*,' said Kippernose, in a joyous whisper. Then he bent down, right down, and got down on his knees to bring his face near to the people.

'Why aren't you running away from me?' he said, softly, so as not to frighten them. 'Why aren't you running away as you always do? Please tell me, I beg of you.'

Jim Surtees was so angry that he had no fear of Kippernose, and he climbed upon his overturned apple-cart, and shouted up at him, 'Why, you great fool, it's because we cannot *smell* you.'

'Smell?' said Kippernose, puzzled.

'Yes; smell, stink, pong, stench; call it what you like,' said Jim.

'But I don't smell,' said Kippernose.

'Oh, yes you do!' all the people shouted together.

'You stink,' shouted Jim. 'You stink to the very heavens. That's why everyone runs away from you. It's too much for us – we just *have* to run away.'

'Why can't you smell me today?' said Kippernose.

'Because we've all caught a cold in the head for the first time in our lives, and our noses are stuffed up and runny, and we cannot smell anything, that's why,' said Jim. 'Some merchant came from England, selling ribbons, and gave us his germs as well. So we cannot smell you today, but next week we'll be better, and then see how we'll run.'

'But what can I do?' said Kippernose, looking so sad that even Jim felt sorry for him.

'I'm so lonely, with no one to talk to.'

'Well, you could take a bath,' said Jim.

'And you could wash your whiskers,' said Mrs Dobson. '. . . and your hair,' she added.

'*And* you could wash your clothes,' said Mr Dobson.

'*And* change your socks,' said Mrs Fox, eyeing his feet.

Distant memories stirred in Kippernose's head. 'Yes. Oh . . . yes. Mother did say something about all that, once, long ago; but I didn't take much notice. Do I really smell as badly as all that? Do I really?'

'Oh yes, you certainly do,' said Mrs Dobson. 'You smell a good deal worse than you can imagine. You turned my cheese green last week, *and* made Mrs Hill's baby cry for two hours without stopping when she left a window open by mistake. Oh, yes, you smell badly, Kippernose, as badly as anything could smell in this world.'

'If I do all you say, if I get all neat and clean, will you stop running away and be friends?' said Kippernose.

'Of course we will,' said Jim Surtees. 'We have nothing against giants. They can be useful if only they'll look where they're putting their feet and they do say the giants were the best story-tellers in the old days.'

'Just you wait and see,' shouted Kippernose. As soon as he had filled his shopping basket,

he walked purposefully off towards the hills. In his basket were one hundred and twenty bars of soap, and fifty bottles of bubble-bath!

That night Kippernose was busy as never before. Fires roared, and hot water gurgled in all the pipes of his house. There was such a steaming, and a splashing, and a gasping, and a bubbling, and a lathering, and a singing, and a laughing, as had not been heard in Kippernose's house for a hundred years. A smell of soap and bubble-bath drifted out upon the air, and even as far away as the town, people caught a whiff of it.

'What's that lovely smell?' said Mrs Dobson to her husband. 'There's a beautifully clean and scented smell, that makes me think of a summer garden, even though it is the middle of winter.'

Then there was a bonfire of dirty old clothes in a field near Kippernose's farm, and a snip-snipping of hair and whiskers. Then there was a great rummaging in drawers and cupboards, and a shaking and airing of fresh clothes. The whole of that week, Kippernose was busy, so busy that he almost forgot to sleep and eat.

When Friday came round again, the people of the town saw an astonishing sight. Dressed in a neat Sunday suit, clean and clipped, shining in the wintry sun, and smelling of soap and sweet lavender, Kippernose strode towards them. He was a new Kippernose. The people crowded round him, and Jim Surtees shouted, 'Is it really you, Kippernose?'

'It certainly is,' said Kippernose, beaming joyously.

'Then you're welcome amongst us,' said Jim. 'You smell as sweetly as a flower, indeed you do, and I never thought you'd do it. Three cheers for good old Kippernose! Hip. Hip.'

And the crowd cheered, 'Hooray! Hooray! Hooray!'

Kippernose was never short of friends after that. He was so good and kind that all the people loved him, and he became the happiest giant in all the world.

Ever afterwards, if any children would not go in the bath, or wash, or brush their teeth, or have their hair cut ... then their mothers would tell them the story of Giant Kippernose.

Rabbit and Lark

James Reeves

'Under the ground
   It's rumbly and dark
And interesting,'
   Said Rabbit to Lark.

Said Lark to Rabbit,
   'Up in the sky
There's plenty of room
   And it's airy and high.'

'Under the ground
   It's warm and dry.
Won't you live with me?'
   Was Rabbit's reply.

'The air's so sunny.
   I wish you'd agree,'
Said the little Lark,
   'To live with me.'

But under the ground
   And up in the sky,
Larks can't burrow
   Nor rabbits fly.

74

So Skylark over
    And Rabbit under
They had to settle
    To live asunder.

And often these two friends
    Meet with a will
For a chat together
    On top of the hill.

How the Elephant Became

Ted Hughes

The unhappiest of all the creatures was Bombo. Bombo didn't know what to become. At one time he thought he might make a fairly good horse. At another time he thought that perhaps he was meant to be a kind of bull. But it was no good. Not only the horses, but all the other creatures too, gathered to laugh at him when he tried to be a horse. And when he tried to be a bull, the bulls just walked away shaking their heads.

'Be yourself,' they all said.

Bombo sighed. That's all he ever heard: 'Be yourself. Be yourself.' What was himself? That's what he wanted to know.

So most of the time he just stood, with sad eyes, letting the wind blow his ears this way and that, while the other creatures raced around him and above him, perfecting themselves.

'I'm just stupid,' he said to himself. 'Just stupid and slow and I shall never become anything.'

That was his main trouble, he felt sure. He was much too slow and clumsy – and so big!

None of the other creatures were anywhere near so big. He searched hard to find another creature as big as he was, but there was not one. This made him feel all the more silly and in the way.

But this was not all. He had great ears that flapped and hung, and a long, long nose. His nose was useful. He could pick things up with it. But none of the other creatures had a nose anything like it. They all had small neat noses, and they laughed at his. In fact, with that, and his ears, and his long white sticking-out tusks, he was a sight.

As he stood, there was a sudden thunder of hooves. Bombo looked up in alarm.

'Aside, aside, aside!' roared a huge voice. 'We're going down to drink.'

Bombo managed to force his way backwards into a painful clump of thorn-bushes, just in time to let Buffalo charge past with all his family. Their long black bodies shone, their curved horns tossed, their tails screwed and curled, as they pounded down towards the water in a cloud of dust. The earth shook under them.

'There's no doubt,' said Bombo, 'who they are. If only I could be as sure of what I am as Buffalo is of what he is.'

Then he pulled himself together.

'To be myself,' he said aloud, 'I shall have to do something that no other creature does.

Lion roars and pounces, and Buffalo charges up and down bellowing. Each of these creatures does something that no other creature does. So. What shall I do?'

He thought hard for a minute.

Then he lay down, rolled over on to his back, and waved his four great legs in the air. After that he stood on his head and lifted his hind legs straight up as if he were going to sunburn the soles of his feet. From this position, he lowered himself back on to his four feet, stood up and looked round. The others should soon get to know me by that, he thought.

Nobody was in sight, so he waited until a pack of wolves appeared on the horizon. Then he began again. On to his back, his legs in the air, then on to his head, and his hind legs straight up.

'Phew!' he grunted, as he lowered himself. 'I shall need some practice before I can keep this up for long.'

When he stood up and looked round him this second time, he got a shock. All the animals were round him in a ring, rolling on their sides with laughter.

'Do it again! Oh, do it again!' they were crying, as they rolled and laughed. 'Do it again, Oh, I shall die with laughter. Oh, my sides, my sides!'

Bombo stared at them in horror.

After a few minutes the laughter died down.

'Come on!' roared Lion. 'Do it again and make us laugh. You look so silly when you do it.'

But Bombo just stood. This was much worse than imitating some other animal. He had never made them laugh so much before.

He sat down and pretended to be inspecting one of his feet, as if he were alone. And, one by one, now that there was nothing to laugh at, the other animals walked away, still chuckling over what they had seen.

'Next show same time tomorrow!' shouted Fox, and they all burst out laughing again.

Bombo sat, playing with his foot, letting the tears trickle down his long nose.

Well, he'd had enough. He'd tried to be himself, and all the animals had laughed at him.

That night he waded out to a small island in the middle of the great river that ran through the forest. And there, from then on, Bombo lived alone, seen by nobody but the little birds and a few beetles.

One night, many years later, Parrot suddenly screamed and flew up into the air above the trees. All his feathers were singed. The forest was on fire.

Within a few minutes, the animals were running for their lives. Jaguar, Wolf, Stag, Cow, Bear, Sheep, Cockerel, Mouse, Giraffe – all were running side by side and jumping over each other to get away from the flames. Behind them, the fire came through the treetops like a terrific red wind.

'Oh dear! Oh dear! Our houses, our children!' cried the animals.

Lion and Buffalo were running along with the rest.

'The fire will go as far as the forest goes, and the forest goes on for ever,' they cried, and ran with sparks falling into their hair. On and on they ran, hour after hour, and all they could hear was the thunder of the fire at their tails.

On into the middle of the next day, and still they were running.

At last they came to the wide, deep, swift river. They could go no farther. Behind them the fire boomed as it leapt from tree to tree. Smoke lay so thickly over the forest and the river that the sun could not be seen. The animals floundered in the shallows at the river's edge, trampling the banks to mud, treading on each other, coughing and sneezing in the white ashes that were falling thicker than thick snow out of the cloud of smoke. Fox sat on Sheep and Sheep sat on Rhinoceros.

They all set up a terrible roaring, wailing, crying, howling, moaning sound. It seemed like the end of the animals. The fire came nearer, bending over them like a thundering

roof, while the black river swirled and rum-
bled beside them.

Out on his island stood Bombo, admiring
the fire which made a fine sight through the
smoke with its high spikes of red flame. He
knew he was quite safe on his island. The fire
couldn't cross that great stretch of water very
easily.

At first he didn't see the animals crowding
low by the edge of the water. The smoke and
ash were too thick in the air. But soon he heard
them. He recognised Lion's voice shouting:

'Keep ducking yourselves in the water.
Keep your fur wet and the sparks will not burn
you.'

And the voice of Sheep crying:

'If we duck ourselves we're swept away by
the river.' .

And the other creatures – Gnu, Ferret, Cobra, Partridge, crying:

'We must drown or burn. Good-bye, brothers and sisters!'

It certainly did seem like the end of the animals.

Without a pause, Bombo pushed his way into the water. The river was deep, the current heavy and fierce, but Bombo's legs were both long and strong. Burnt trees, that had fallen into the river higher up and were drifting down, banged against him, but he hardly felt them.

In a few minutes he was coming up into shallow water towards the animals. He was almost too late. The flames were forcing them, step by step, into the river, where the current was snatching them away.

Lion was sitting on Buffalo, Wolf was sitting on Lion, Wildcat on Wolf, Badger on Wildcat, Cockerel on Badger, Rat on Cockerel, Weasel on Rat, Lizard on Weasel, Tree-Creeper on Lizard, Harvest Mouse on Tree-Creeper, Beetle on Harvest Mouse, Wasp on Beetle, and on top of Wasp, Ant, gazing at the raging flames through his spectacles and covering his ears from their roar.

When the animals saw Bombo looming through the smoke, a great shout went up:

'It's Bombo! It's Bombo!'

All the animals took up the cry:

'Bombo! Bombo!'

Bombo kept coming closer. As he came, he sucked up water in his long silly nose and squirted it over his back, to protect himself from the heat and the sparks. Then, with the same long, silly nose he reached out and began to pick up the animals, one by one, and seat them on his back.

'Take us!' cried Mole.

'Take us!' cried Monkey.

He loaded his back with the creatures that had hooves and big feet; then he told the little clinging things to climb on to the great folds of his ears. Soon he had every single creature aboard. Then he turned and began to wade back across the river, carrying all the animals of the forest towards safety.

Once they were safe on the island they danced for joy. Then they sat down to watch the fire. Suddenly Mouse gave a shout:

'Look! The wind is bringing sparks across the river. The sparks are blowing into the island trees. We shall burn here too.'

As he spoke, one of the trees on the edge of the island crackled into flames. The animals set up a great cry and began to run in all directions.

'Help! Help! Help! We shall burn here too!'

But Bombo was ready. He put those long silly tusks of his, that he had once been so ashamed of, under the roots of the burning tree and heaved it into the river. He threw every tree into the river till the island was bare. The sparks now fell on to the bare torn ground, where the animals trod them out easily. Bombo had saved them again.

Next morning the fire had died out at the river's edge. The animals on the island looked across at the smoking, blackened plain where the forest had been. Then they looked round for Bombo.

He was nowhere to be seen.

'Bombo!' they shouted. 'Bombo!' And listened to the echo.

But he had gone.

He is still very hard to find. Though he is huge and strong, he is very quiet.

But what did become of him in the end? Where is he now?

Ask any of the animals, and they will tell you:

'Though he is shy, he is the strongest, the cleverest, and the kindest of all the animals. He can carry anything and he can push anything down. He can pick you up in his nose and wave you in the air. We would make him our king if we could get him to wear a crown.'

Lisa's Best Friend

June Crebbin

Lisa's best friend was the Giant. She had known him for a very long time. Ever since she was four years old, just after Andrew was born.

The Giant went everywhere with her. He sat next to her at the dining table. He slept on the floor beside her bed and he always played in the garden with her.

Whenever they went to the park, people would stop and chat to Lisa's Mummy or Daddy and coo over Andrew. So Lisa talked to the Giant. He was always there when she needed him. Together they climbed on the wooden climbing frame. They played on the roundabouts and swings.

Sometimes, when Lisa was flying nearer and nearer to the sky, Mummy would call: 'That's high enough, Lisa. Don't swing any higher.' Then Lisa would reply: 'I can't help it. The Giant is pushing me. He's very strong.'

And sometimes, just as it was bedtime, Lisa would remember that she had promised to help the Giant with the huge hole they were digging in the garden. Then Daddy would get cross and once he said: 'That Giant is getting much too big for his boots. That Giant will have to go.' Lisa had covered the Giant's ears quickly so that he wouldn't hear such a dreadful thing and the two of them had gone upstairs and played a game in the bedroom before going to sleep.

Still, on the whole, Lisa and the Giant managed to stay out of trouble. That is, until the night before Lisa started school.

Everything was ready. Her clothes were laid out neatly on the chair beside her bed. Her school-bag was packed with pencils and crayons and a rubber. Her PE kit was in its own bag with her name on. Lisa Brown was ready.

Then she thought of something.

'The Giant hasn't got his things ready,' she said.

'That's because he's not going,' said Mummy firmly, tucking Lisa into bed. She gave her a kiss. 'There'll be quite enough children in the class without the Giant.'

Lisa sat up. 'Then I'm not going,' she said.

'Don't be silly,' said Mummy. 'There'll be lots of children to play with. You won't need the Giant.'

'I will,' said Lisa.

'I'll look after him,' said Mummy.

'No,' said Lisa. 'He'll be lonely without me.'

'I'll take him to the shops,' said Mummy.

'What are you doing when I'm at school?' said Lisa. 'Tell me again.'

'Well,' said Mummy, sitting down on the bed so that she could give Lisa a cuddle, 'first of all you and Andrew and I are all going to school. Then I'll take Andrew to the shops. Then we'll come home to do the washing and then it will be dinner-time and time to meet you.'

'Then the Giant will have to come to school with me,' decided Lisa. 'He doesn't like shopping. He doesn't like washing and he doesn't like Andrew.'

So the next morning, when Lisa went to school, the Giant went with her. He was very good. He sat very still when the teacher told them a story. In the afternoon, he wanted to paint a picture of the house where he lived. But of course he was much too big to hold the brush so Lisa painted the picture for him.

'It's lovely,' said Mummy when Lisa took it home.

'Don't let Andrew touch it,' said Lisa. 'If he dribbles on it, the Giant will be very angry.'

Daddy admired the picture when he came home. He looked at it very carefully. He liked the garden and the trees. He liked the fence and the gate. He liked the sky and the birds. At the bottom there was some writing.

'That says Lisa,' said Lisa.

'I know,' said Daddy. 'It's very good.'

'The teacher didn't know how to write the Giant,' explained Lisa. So Daddy wrote it for her. Then he pinned it right at the top of the cupboard in the kitchen, well out of Andrew's way and where everyone could see it.

'Are you going to paint another picture tomorrow?' he said.

'We might,' said Lisa. 'I don't know if the Giant's thought of one yet.'

The next day at school, Lisa played in the Wendy House. The teacher said four children could play in the Wendy House. She chose Michael, Rakesh, Joanna and Lisa. The Giant wanted to play in the Wendy House too. But of course he was much too big so he had to wait outside.

Lisa and Joanna and Michael and Rakesh played cops and robbers. Lisa and Michael and Rakesh lay fast asleep inside the Wendy House and Joanna climbed in through the window and jumped on them. Then they played tea-parties and babies.

'Have you got a baby at home?' said Joanna, as she arranged tiny cups and saucers on the table. 'I haven't.'

'Yes,' said Lisa, and she told Joanna all about Andrew, how he kept tumbling over because he was only just learning to walk, how he smiled and smiled when Lisa came home from school, and how he always went to bed at six o'clock and Lisa went to bed at seven o'clock.

'I wish I had a baby,' said Joanna.

Daddy met Lisa after school that day. Andrew was there too.

'Where's Mummy?' said Lisa.

'You remember,' said Daddy. 'She's at work today. Shall we go to the park?'

Lisa played on the roundabouts and swings. Daddy offered to push her. But Lisa could go really high all by herself. She knew how to tuck her legs underneath the seat of the swing when she came down and push them straight out in front when she went up. Higher and higher she flew. 'I'm nearly touching the sky!' she shouted.

'What did you do at school today?' said Daddy on the way home.

'I didn't paint a picture,' said Lisa. 'But I might tomorrow. Joanna and I might paint a picture together.'

'Who's Joanna?' said Daddy.

'She's in my class,' said Lisa, 'and she hasn't any baby brothers or sisters.'

Lisa played with Joanna at playtimes and in the Wendy House. She sat next to her on the carpet when they had a story and she always chose her for a partner in PE. Joanna was very good at jumping high into the air. She thought Lisa was very good at hopping. They were both good at throwing the bean bag to each other and catching it. They were the best in the class. They had to do it on their own to show the others and they didn't drop it once.

That was the day Joanna went home for tea with Lisa. The two girls arranged it at playtime.

'Will I be able to play with your baby?' said Joanna.

'Yes,' said Lisa, 'and I'll show you my garden and my bicycle.'

After school, at the school gates, Lisa asked her mother if Joanna could come for tea and Joanna asked her mother if she could go to Lisa's for tea. So the two mothers met and chatted and agreed.

Joanna was allowed to push the pram all the way home, but Lisa helped her up and down the kerbs which were a bit tricky if you weren't used to them.

They stopped off at the park for a while. They played on the swings and the roundabouts. They climbed all over the climbing frame. But they liked the see-saw best.

When they got home, Joanna played with Andrew in the living room and Mummy called Lisa to help her in the kitchen. She was putting plates and dishes onto the table.

'Where do you think Joanna should sit?' she said.

'Next to me,' said Lisa.

'But what about the Giant?' said Mummy. 'Doesn't he want any tea today?'

'No,' said Lisa.

'Well,' said Mummy, 'and I've made a cho–colate cake specially too.' She lifted it out of its tin and put it on a blue plate in the middle of the table.

'The Giant had to go,' said Lisa. 'He said he was going back to his own land. He was getting much too big for his boots.'

'In that case,' said Mummy, 'you'd better ask Joanna if she likes chocolate cake.'

Joanna did. She liked banana sandwiches and ice-cream and lemonade too. She liked everything.

When Daddy came home, he came straight into the kitchen.

'Any pictures today?' he said. Then he said, 'Hello, I thought I only had one little girl in my family. I must be seeing things.'

'Don't be silly Daddy,' said Lisa. 'This is Joanna. Joanna is my best friend.'

That's my dog!

Joan Poulson

Mum took me to the Dogs' Home
on my birthday. I'd waited
years, it seemed, for the day
to arrive. We went inside.

There were dogs of all sizes –
long-eared and short, in every
dog-colour you'd imagine. They
jumped up at the wire, barking
a plea 'Choose me to take
home! Choose me! Take me!'
All of them, that is, but one.

They were lively, bright-eyed
with wagging tails that said
'It's *me* you want beside you
when you go for walks, to lie
next to your bed, protect you
in the park. *I'll* be your
mate, search your room before
you go in when it's dark.'
All of them, that is, but him.

He lay watching from the back
of the run, black ears
drooped over big brown eyes
shivering, afraid, half the
size of any of the others.

Then I saw on his face
that look I knew from
my mirror – look that says
'I'm quiet, not brave, nothing
special in any way. But I'm
stronger than I seem, would
love to have a friend, someone
I can trust. I'd gladly share in
bad days – and make others full
of fun.' I winked at him, grinned
up at Mum. And firmly said
'That's my dog! That's the one!'

The Lost Boy

Alison Uttley

One day Sam Pig was walking in the woods
when he came across a little lost boy. Sam
could hear the little snuffly noises, and the
crackling of sticks, and he went warily, for,
of course, it might have been a wolf, or a
gamekeeper or even the fox. He peered round
the tree and crept softly through the brambles,
scratching his legs and tearing his trousers even
worse than usual. Then he saw him. There sat
the little, lost boy with tears trickling down
his cheeks and his wide, blue eyes brimming
with water. Sam watched the little boy for
a while and tears came to his own eyes in sym-
pathy, but he couldn't cry as easily as little
boys cry. He saw the child fumble in his pock-
ets and shake them inside out. Sam was much
excited when this happened but all the little
boy brought out was a small mouth organ.
He put it to his lips and made a short wail
of music, then he dropped it on the grass and
leaned over like a bundle of misery, sobbing
quietly. He put his arms around his head and
curled up in a ball, with the mouth organ as
a pillow.

How Sam stared! He crept close and squatted by the little boy's side, watching that wet, sleepy face, waiting for the child to awake. Overhead a robin sang, and fluttered its wings and fluffed out its red breast. Then down it hopped to a low bush. It began to sing again and Sam, who, of course, knew the language of birds, listened to the words of the song. It was warbling a carol called 'The Babes in the Wood'.

> '*These pretty babes went hand in hand,*
> *Went wandering up and down:*
> *But never more could see the man*
> *Approaching from the town.*
> *Their pretty lips with blackberries*
> *Were all besmeared and dyed;*
> *And when they saw the darksome night*
> *They sat them down and cried.*'

The carol was about two children who were lost long ago and covered with leaves by the robins.

The robin picked a leaf and dropped it on the little boy's face, on his lips which were stained with blackberries just like the boy's in the story. Then it began to drop leaves on Sam Pig.

'Steady on!' exclaimed Sam in a gruff whisper as the leaves fluttered down. 'I'm not a Babe in the Wood, I'm not lost.'

'But this boy is,' sang the robin. 'Help me to cover him with leaves, Sam.'

So Sam and the robin spread a nice quilt of autumn leaves over the little boy to keep him warm.

At last the child stirred in his sleep and stretched out a hand which Sam licked with his own warm tongue. Then he awoke and sat up, shaking the leaves away and staring at Sam Pig.

'Had a good sleep?' asked Sam, kindly.

'Hallo,' said the little boy slowly. 'Who are you? I want to go home.'

'I'll take care of you,' said Sam. He pulled out a dirty handkerchief and wiped the little boy's face, making it even dirtier with the wood ashes and mud.

'There, you look better,' said Sam, admiring him. 'I'm Sam Pig. What's your name?'

'Jack Hickory. My father's a thatcher, and he's been thatching Farmer Greensleeves' haystacks, and I started off home alone. I got losted in the wood. I want to go home to my mammy.'

'Well, come along with me,' said Sam. 'I may be only a small pig, but I'm a bold one. I'm not afraid of foxes or bears. I'll take you home.'

So little Sam Pig trotted over the woodland and little Jack Hickory skipped along beside him. Sam took out his pipe and played a tune and the little boy enjoyed the music.

'My Dad can play a mouth organ,' said he, 'and he can play a tune on a straw, and he can whistle.'

'I can whistle,' said Sam, 'and Brock can play a mouth organ and I can play a fiddle.'

Jack handed his mouth organ to Sam and Sam squeaked up and down trying to make a tune.

'What have you got in that bag?' asked Jack, pointing to the satchel on Sam's back.

Sam hitched the bag round and opened it. 'Half a loaf of new bread and a piece of honeycomb. I always take provisions with me when I am going on adventure. Here, take a bite.' Sam broke off some bread and put a piece of honeycomb on the top and Jack ate it hungrily. They drank some water from the clear stream and as Sam raised his head he saw Brock the Badger looking at him from behind a bush.

'Oh, Brock! Come here and see a little lost boy. I'm bringing him home to us,' cried Sam. Brock came from his shelter and held out his paw to the child and Jack took it and kept it in his own small, warm hand.

'You're like a bear,' he told Brock. 'I'm not afraid of you.'

'No need to be,' said Brock. 'You can come home with us and see where we live. We've never had a boy in our house, yet.'

So the little boy went home with Sam Pig and he liked the house so much he did not want to go away.

'You needn't wash,' said Sam. 'I often don't wash my paws and although Ann, my sister, is very particular she doesn't notice me.'

'I'm glad of that,' said the little boy.

'And you can eat as much as ever you want. Lots of honeycomb and bread and butter and soup,' added Sam.

'Just what I like,' said the little boy. 'Do you have lollipops and ice-cream?'

'No, only ice-cream in winter when Jack Frost comes to the streams and makes it for us,' said Sam. 'And our lollipops are the sweet stems of blackberry bushes. But you can get your feet wet and it doesn't matter.'

So at night the little boy sat by the fire next to Sam Pig and he ate hot roast potatoes with butter and milk, and he went to bed on straw, wrapped in a blanket, next to Sam on the floor.

In the middle of the night he awoke and he lay listening to the snores all around him. Brock was snoring loudly, like an organ, sitting in his chair, not really asleep, and the four pigs were squeaking and grunting like a chorus of bagpipes. It made the little boy laugh and he turned over and curled up close to Sam.

Brock the Badger waked him the next day. 'Be off, you two little 'uns, and wash yourselves.'

'Wash? Sam said I needn't wash,' protested Jack sleepily.

'But I say you must,' said Brock, sternly. 'Go out and dip your head in the stream and splash your eyes to see well, both of you.'

A very wet little boy came back to the table, for there was no towel by the icy cold stream.

Ann threw a brown straw rag to him and he dried himself as well as possible and rubbed himself with bracken, but Sam leapt about without any towel at all. They dressed quickly and ran hungrily to have breakfast.

Tom Pig had cooked a dish of porridge, and the little boy held out his wooden bowl.

'I have porridge at home,' said he, 'and then I have an egg.'

'No eggs for you here,' said Brock. 'You must eat more porridge. We only have eggs for tea or for birthdays or Christmas.'

'But you can have a mug of milk and some honeycomb and bread,' added Ann, who was sorry for the little boy, so clean and so white and so pretty among the brown sturdy little pigs and Brock the Badger.

'I like a little boy,' said Ann. 'You can have my honeycomb, too,' she added.

'I 'spects my mother and father will come looking for me,' said the little boy.

'They won't find you here,' said Tom. 'This house is invisible when Brock wants it to be. He doesn't like mothers and fathers.'

'We have to live invisibly,' explained Ann, calmly. 'Farmer Greensleeves knows about us but nobody else except animals unless we want them to know.'

'I'll show you the dragon,' said Sam. 'And the water-maid and the river.'

So when the washing-up was done and the beds were made and the straw shaken and the house swept clean and the mat beaten at the door, Sam Pig and Ann with the small boy between them galloped off to the woods. They shouted and laughed as they ran. There lay a great brown stone, covered with moss and lichens, deep in the ferns and forget-me-nots.

Sam leapt on its back and Jack followed him, while Ann stood near stroking the stone and removing some of the greenery and tiny ferns which grew in the cracks.

'Can you feel anything?' whispered Sam.

'No,' said the little boy, softly.

'Can't you feel it breathe?' asked Ann.

The little boy held his breath. His eyes were startled. He stooped to the stone and touched it with timid fingers. Yes, he thought he could feel just the gentlest breath, a slow up-and-down movement, as if the earth itself was breathing.

'It's the dragon. He's asleep,' whispered Sam.

'Can you wake him?' asked Jack.

'No, for he might eat you. He ate a cow the last time he was awake, and he kept us busy trying to feed him,' said Ann.

'Where are his eyes?' asked the boy.

'Here,' said Ann, 'I've been uncovering them.' She showed Jack two narrow slits through which he could see a dark crystalline sparkle. Then a larger slit in the stone seemed to move and a great mouth slowly opened and a set of sharp, brown, stony teeth was shown. The dragon yawned and sent out a puff of smoke blue as the forget-me-nots. Then it snuggled down in the undergrowth so that Sam and the little boy fell off and rolled away. The dragon lay very still, fast asleep.

'Oh, dear, we nearly wakened him,' cried Ann with a tremor.

They ran away, but when they were on the edge of the wood they all turned round. The stone lay very still, the dragon was safe for perhaps a thousand years.

'Now let's go to the river,' said Sam. 'Can you swim?'

'Oh, yes,' cried Jack. 'My father taught me.'

'We can swim, too, but not very well,' said Ann, laughing. 'We'll dive in and look for the water-maiden. She sometimes sits on a rock and plays a little harp.'

'But we have to be quiet or the river won't like it,' added Sam. 'Old Man River gets very fierce with us.'

They undressed and leapt into the rushing river, and swam about the rocks in the pools. It was so clear the little boy could see the bottom and down there he spied a small golden looking-glass. He dropped to the sandy bottom and brought it up.

'Look what I've found,' he cried.

'Oh, it belongs to the water-maid,' said Sam. They all climbed on the green, mossy rock and the little boy waved the glass to catch the sun rays and reflect them on the water. In a minute there was a ripple beside them, a white arm came out of the water, and the mirror was taken from the child's hand.

'Thank you, O boy,' said a sweet, soft voice,

high and clear. There below them was a most beautiful girl, with long gold hair and smiling wet face. She held the mirror and sang a water-song to the little boy and the two pigs.

'*Water, dreaming water,*
Here am I, your daughter.
Shall I bring you morning flowers,
Or fountains clear of golden showers?'

Tossing spray over them in a fountain of drops, she dived into the waves and disappeared.

'See, she's left something,' said Jack. He picked up a green, silken scarf which floated near and he wound it round his neck.

'I think she left it for you,' said Ann.

But the water began to growl and roar, it threw a wave at them and washed them off the rock. It sent a bigger wave and drove them from the river to the bank.

'Give me back my daughter's scarf,' growled the river, and, frightened by the tumult, Jack tossed it away. 'It is for no earth-child,' said the river.

They ran as fast as they could over the water-meadow back to the woods.

'The river is cross today,' said Ann. 'I thought the scarf was a present to you, Jack. I didn't know. I'm sorry.'

'We got away just in time,' panted Sam Pig. 'I don't think the river likes humans.'

They strolled through the woods and Sam told the little boy about the trees and the berries and the flowers they saw, and they picked a bunch of flowers. Then they heard footsteps and they hid behind a tree.

'Oh, dear, I wish I could be invisible,' sighed Sam. 'I don't want anyone to see us.'

'It's my father,' cried the little boy, excitedly. 'He's looking for me.'

So Sam dodged away into the background of the woods and the little boy ran forward to grasp his father's hand.

'Oh, Jack! Jack! Where have you been? We've been looking everywhere for you,' cried the man, as he grasped his little son.

'Oh, my Dad,' cried Jack. 'Oh, I've been living with the four pigs and Old Brock the Badger, in a little house with a straw roof.'

'You have, have you?' said his father, picking some wet straws out of the little boy's clothes. 'What did you have to eat? Swill?'

'And we had honeycomb and nice bread and milk,' said Jack. 'And do you know I saw a dragon in the wood and a water-maid in the river.'

'Did ye now!' exclaimed the unbelieving father.

'And I was covered with leaves, just like the tale of "the Babes in the Wood",' continued Jack, skipping along and holding tightly to his father's hand.

'Then you can take me to this pigs' house where you've been stopping,' said his father.

'It's this way,' said the child. Then he stopped, puzzled. 'I can't find it, but there's the dragon.' He pointed out the great stone in the wood.

'That's not a dragon. It's nubbet an old rock,' said his father, and when the little boy pointed out the dragon's eyes and mouth where the ferns had been cleared away, the man would not believe it.

'Here, come along home to your mother. You've been dreaming all this,' said the father.

'I haven't,' said Jack, almost in tears, but he soon forgot his anger as he skipped home.

His mother was more understanding and she listened to his tale of Sam Pig and Brock the Badger.

'You never know,' said she, 'there may be such beings. We don't all of us see everything. Little children have power to see things we have lost, I've heard. I think he has been taken care of by somebody and something, and I am very thankful to Sam Pig.'

Jack took her to the woods the next day and showed her the great stone which he called a dragon. She noticed the bits of moss and ferns which Ann Pig had removed from the slits and she looked closely at the eyes of the stone beast. One eye sparkled and glittered as it watched her, and she thought she saw a wink.

'Put your hand here, Mummy,' said Jack and she laid her warm hand on the backbone of the stone. Surely she felt a slight movement, a breathing of some ancient animal?

Jack took her to the river and she watched the shining glinting water, and she saw the kingfisher flash his wings and the water rat glide softly in the bank. Then did she see the white arm of the water-maiden for a split second? She felt sure she heard the sweet ripple of the harp.

But she could never find Sam Pig's house although she and Jack hunted for weeks, at all times, among the ferns and the forget-me-nots. It was invisible. Only the little mouth organ lay in the wood, where Jack had dropped it.

Friends Again

Paul Rogers

My brother bashed me with a stick.
I hit him with the hose.
He pulled my hair. I scratched his face.
He thumped me on the nose.

I bit his leg; he screamed. *I* screamed.
We called each other names.
Then Mum came out and asked us why
We couldn't play nice games.

I sulked. He moped. I frowned. He smiled.
I let him in my den.
He offered me a sticky sweet.
And now we're friends again.

Stepmother

Margaret Mahy

There was once a princess called Jennifer – but her father called her Jenny – Princess Jenny. (She knew she was a princess because her mother had died when she was quite small – just like Snow White's mother; just like Cinderella's.)

People had read all the fairytale books to Princess Jenny. So she was ready for whatever might come when her father brought her new, young stepmother home (Well – *you* know what stepmothers are supposed to be like – full of wickedness, always changing princesses into frogs or worms or even making them do the housework and sit in the ashes.)

Before Jenny's perhaps stepmother became her real stepmother, they had all gone to the zoo and on picnics together. But, thought Princess Jenny, she won't take *me* by surprise!

The stepmother looked to Jenny like a tall, golden tree. She looked as if beautiful birds might sit on her and sing, or butterflies come to visit her for honey. She looked as if she might break into wild, shining blossoms at the sound of a certain magical word.

'Being beautiful just makes it worse!' she told her small brother, William. 'There is no excuse.'

The very next morning, when her father had gone to work, Princess Jenny got up and put on her best pink frock with the frill, her silver locket and her shiny Christmas crown. She looked at her reflection with satisfaction.

'Hello Princess,' she said to it.

Then she packed her bag. Princess Jenny was running away. She knew she must not run very far away. After all someone had to keep an eye on the stepmother to make sure she didn't enchant William. Fortunately she knew a very good place to run to quite close by.

I shall run to the hole in the hedge by the compost heap and live there, thought Jenny. Stepmothers are too proud to come near a simple compost heap. Besides, there are wasps there. A stepmother wouldn't want to be stung by a wasp. It is lucky that I don't let wasps bother me ... Now to pack the royal treasure.

The royal treasure was particularly royal and rare. There was Clara, and there was Sarah, the Princess's best doll and her second-best doll. There were two fairytale books – *Cinderella* and *Snow White*.

'Plenty in *there* about stepmothers!' said Jenny darkly. She put in her old teddy, although she had not played with him for months. She did not want a stepmother playing with him, or even practising wickedness upon him.

It was still early in the morning, just half-past breakfast, but already the stepmother was up to wickedness. She was pretending to be ordinary – wearing a usual apron over her green dress. She was pretending to put the vacuum cleaner together.

Princess Jenny could see at once that she was doing it the wrong way. The stepmother took one look at Jenny.

'Oh, good morning, Princess,' she said in her lazy voice, as golden and warm as hot buttered toast. 'Where are you off to?'

'A secret place,' said Jenny. 'I can't tell you where, because you'd come and find me.'

'It's best to be on the safe side,' the stepmother agreed. 'I'm glad to see you are a careful princess.'

'You being a stepmother and me a princess –' said Princess Jenny, 'you might turn me *into* something. I've got to watch out.'

'Indeed you have,' the stepmother said firmly. 'In fact, I'm feeling rather wicked at the moment. Run away quickly before I dress you in rags and make you do all the housework.'

Princess Jenny ran out into the sunshine, her suitcase banging against her legs. '*I* could do the housework better than she could,' said

Jenny to herself. 'She doesn't even know how to put the vacuum cleaner together ... I'd have helped her if she'd asked me.'

She scrambled into the hole under the hedge by the compost heap, pulled her suitcase in sideways and unpacked it. Then she sat on it. She sat for a while just getting the feel of being a runaway princess. From under the leaves the hedge looked scratchy. It had a hot smell, like pepper.

'Princesses have a lot to put up with when there are stepmothers around,' Princess Jenny said aloud. 'At any moment now terrible wickedness could start.'

She looked out through the grass stems. The stepmother was bringing William outside with his rocking-horse.

'Well, look at that!' muttered Princess Jenny in disgust. 'See what she's done! She's dressed him in his best clothes. That's his best, blue jersey and his best trousers.' She kept on watching.

After a while the stepmother came out and gave William a banana. Why doesn't she put his bib on? wondered Jenny.

Jenny could not bear to see him have a messy banana when he had his best jersey on. She had to get out of her hole in the hedge and run over the lawn back to the house. The step-mother was in the front room upstairs, prob-ably making beds. The vacuum cleaner was still on the floor. Quickly Princess Jenny put it together properly. She plugged it in but did not switch it on. Then she went to the kitchen drawer where William's bibs were kept, took a clean one and ran outside again. She put it on him, grumbling as she did so.

'Well, *she* doesn't know much. Banana makes brownish stains which don't come out. You've got to be careful with banana.'

Then she ran back and climbed into the hedge again and straightened her crown. 'Princess of leaves and birds' nests!' she said, nodding to the teddy bear.

The stepmother came out of the house. She rocked William on his rocking-horse and then started to look around the yard. You could see she was searching for something.

'Looking for me!' Princess Jenny said, sitting still behind the leaves, trying to breathe softly. The stepmother was talking to herself.

'Where can it be?' she was saying. 'There must be some, somewhere. Every garden has parsley.'

Parsley, thought Princess Jenny. That's a magical plant. I read about it in some fairytale book. You could use it in all sorts of enchantment . . . She's making *spells* already, and it isn't even lunchtime yet!

The stepmother wandered on while Jenny watched her keenly. As the stepmother came to the big patch of parsley, Princess Jenny held her breath ... but the stepmother wandered past it.

'Well,' said Jenny, 'she can't be a very good stepmother. Not at witchcraft! She didn't even *see* that parsley.'

The stepmother went on around the corner of the house, looking as tall and golden as a daffodil. Princess Jenny scrambled out of her hole in the hedge. Mouse-quick, mouse-quiet, she picked several stems of parsley, ran past William and his rocking-horse, put the parsley on the step and then ran back to the hole in the hedge by the compost heap.

'That will show her I'm not afraid of her!' said Princess Jenny, panting a little. 'I'll bet *that* surprises her.' She peered out, almost giggling at the joke. The stepmother came back with some letters in her hand. She stopped, picked up the parsley and went inside without turning around.

Princess Jenny, snug in the hedge, did not see the stepmother again for some time. In a way it made things dull. A stepmother should be more exciting. Besides, she had not hung the washing out yet. Princess Jenny waited and waited. She heard the vacuum cleaner going and then there was silence. No stepmother – no washing.

A stepmother shouldn't be dirty, Jenny thought. I wonder if she has started the washing yet? Mrs McKinnon used to hang it out

early. (Mrs McKinnon was the housekeeper who had come to look after Princess Jenny and little William in the good old days before the stepmother had arrived.)

A moment later a terrible thing happened. The stepmother came out with a rug and a book and a bowl of cherries. She spread the rug on the lawn and sat on it. She began to read. Jenny had never seen such a thing. William saw the cherries and came and sat with her. He put his empty banana skin on his head like a hat and laughed. The stepmother laughed too. She did not make him take it off. Jenny stared and stared.

'She's reading!' Jenny whispered to her

teddy. 'She's reading and laughing and the washing isn't even out yet.'

It was too much. Princess Jenny took her dolls and teddy and wriggled out from the hole under the hedge by the compost heap. She came up to the rug on quiet feet, but the stepmother turned and smiled at her.

'You are looking fierce,' said the stepmother. 'Have some cherries. They are good for fierceness.'

'I am *feeling* fierce,' Jenny cried. 'Things are not being done right.' She paused for breath. 'Why are you reading when the washing isn't hung out? Why didn't you put William's bib on him?'

'Well, I looked at the washing,' said the stepmother, 'but as there was only a little bit, I thought it might be more fun to sit in the sun with William and eat cherries.'

'But you can't do things just because they are fun,' said Princess Jenny loftily. 'You have to be serious and clean about things.'

'Sometimes I am serious,' said the stepmother, 'but it is too fine outdoors today to be serious all the time.'

'It is also a good day for drying washing,' Princess Jenny told her sternly, but the stepmother merely held out the cherries and smiled. William took a fat handful. Princess Jenny had to have some quickly or they would all be gone.

They sat in the sun and ate cherries. It felt funny to be doing such a lazy thing on a week-day morning.

Princess Jenny said shyly, 'Your dress is pretty. I haven't got a green dress.'

'Would you like one?' asked the stepmother. 'I'm not a very good washerwoman, but I'm good at sewing. I will make you a green dress and I will embroider a sunflower on its skirt.'

'You also are not very good as a step-mother,' Princess Jenny said suddenly. 'You should be getting up to wickedness, not doing kind deeds.'

'The fact is,' said the stepmother, 'it is too nice a day to be wicked ... The fact is, I am not really wicked at all. I am too lazy to be wicked.'

'A *kind* stepmother,' muttered Princess Jenny to herself, trying the words out to see how they sounded. Then she looked at the ground and began to grin.

'I'm not really a princess,' she said and took off her crown. 'Having a stepmother made me think I might be one.'

'Have some more cherries,' said the step-mother. 'Do you know, I have missed you all morning. I am not a good housewife. I need lots of help and advice.'

'I put the vacuum cleaner together for you and put William's bib on him,' Jenny remarked, looking pleased with herself.

'I was very impressed,' the stepmother replied. 'But now I need more help. I thought we might have a party tonight – just a little one.'

'Daddy loves a roast dinner,' Jenny said quickly. 'Roast dinner is a family dinner. And Daddy loves ice-cream with chocolate sauce and fruit salad.'

'Good – that is what I wanted to know,' said the stepmother. 'And I thought we could make a cake and ice it and write all our names on. 'John' for your father, and 'William' and 'Jennifer' and 'Anna'. Jenny, you know that Anna is *my* name. Why don't you call me Anna? I'm sure you can if you try.'

'Anna,' said Jenny in a different voice.

'You do say it nicely,' Anna said. 'I've always liked my name, but nobody makes it sound better than you do.'

'Anna and Jennifer, both in green dresses and pretty aprons, cooking a roast dinner,' Jenny said, trying the idea out in words. 'Jenny – I mean Jennifer – helping Anna to look after the house.' She made up her mind that now she was not a princess, she would be Jennifer, green and gold like a daffodil. The wicked step-mother seemed far away – a hundred years ago. Anna and Jennifer hung the last of the cherries over their ears for earrings and began to plan the party as they sat in the sun.

Foot Note

Tony Bradman

I'll tell you a secret
You mustn't repeat,
A secret about
My best friend's . . . feet.
I'm sorry to say
That my friend Ray's
Got feet that smell.
Oh, please don't tell –
He's a very good friend.
But his feet are . . .

                            the end.

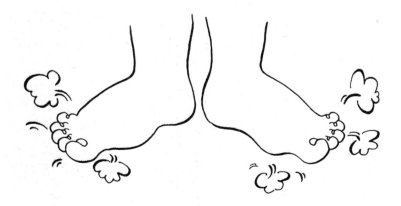

Acknowledgements

The editor and publishers gratefully acknowledge permission to reproduce the following copyright material in this anthology:

'St Pancras and King's Cross' from *Time and Again Stories* (Methuen Children's Books) reprinted by permission of Donald Bisset; 'Foot Note' reprinted by permission of Rogers, Coleridge and White Ltd from *Smile Please* by Tony Bradman first published by Viking Kestrel, 1987, copyright © Tony Bradman, 1987; 'Gloria Who Might Be My Best Friend' reprinted by permission of Victor Gollancz Ltd from *The Julian Stories* by Ann Cameron; 'Finding a Friend' and 'Lisa's Best Friend' copyright © June Crebbin, 1990; 'Giant Kippernose' reprinted by permission of André Deutsch Limited from *Giant Kippernose and Other Stories* by John Cunliffe first published in 1972; 'The Boy in the Garden' copyright © Berlie Doherty, 1990; 'Nittle and Bubberlink' reprinted by permission of Lutterworth Press from *Whispers From a Wardrobe* by Richard Edwards, first published 1987; 'Harry and Amanda' copyright © Adèle Geras, 1990; 'Littlenose Meets Two-Eyes' reprinted by permission of John Grant from his book *The Adventures of Littlenose* first published by the British Broadcasting Corporation in 1972; 'How the Elephant Became' reprinted by permission of Faber and Faber Ltd from *How the Whale Became and Other Stories* by Ted Hughes first published 1963; 'Mr Greentoe's Crocodile' copyright © Jean Kenward, 1990; 'Stepmother' reprinted by permission of J. M. Dent & Sons Ltd from *Leaf Magic* by Margaret Mahy; 'The Toothball' copyright © 1987 Philippa Pearce from *The Toothball*, Andre Deutsch, permission granted by the author; 'That's My Dog' by Joan Poulson from *Toughie Toffee* published in Fontana Lions, 1989; 'Copycat' from *Ask a Silly Question* by Irene Rawnsley, first published in 1988 by Methuen Children's Books; 'Rabbit and Lark' copyright © James Reeves from *The Wandering Moon and Other Poems* (Puffin Books) by James Reeves, reprinted by permission of the James Reeves Estate; 'Friends Again' copyright © Paul Rogers, 1990; 'The Lost Boy' reprinted by permission of Faber and Faber Ltd from *Sam Pig goes to the Seaside* by Alison Uttley first published 1960; 'My Party' reprinted by permission of Collins Publishers from *Rabbiting On* by Kit Wright, first published in Fontana Lions 1978.

Every effort has been made to trace copyright holders. The editor and publishers would like to hear from any copyright holders not acknowledged.